To my son, John III,

May you soon discover that

Sandi's strength is in

your D.N.A.

Published by Lightswitch Learning
250 East 54th Street, Suite 8A, New York, New York 10022
www.lightswitchlearning.com

Educators and Librarians, for a variety of teaching resources, visit www.lightswitchlearning.com

Library of Congress Cataloging-in-Publication Data is available upon request
Library of Congress Catalog Card Number pending

ISBN 978-1-61717-886-3 (hardcover)

The Emancipation of Grandpa Sandy Wills by Cheryl Wills
Illustrated by Randell Pearson

Book design by Randell Pearson, Pearson Designs
The text of this book is set in Minion Pro

Printed in Malaysia

THE EMANCIPATION OF GRANDPA SANDY WILLS

CHERYL WILLS

ILLUSTRATED BY RANDELL PEARSON

Mama crying. White flowers on the casket. The funeral director calling it a "celebration of life."

Nothing we did that day could bring Daddy back. Clarence Wills, 38, father of five, had died in a motorcycle accident. And at 13, I had lost the bravest father any child could want.

He was also mysterious. All I knew was that my dad was a firefighter and that he was born in Tennessee. He hadn't talked much about his side of the family. *Who were the other Wills on my family tree?*

That question still haunted me thirty years later. Sure, as a popular TV news anchor in New York City I had interviewed hundreds of people, but I needed to know who *I* was.

One day I came home and searched a genealogy website that helps people learn about their ancestors. I entered my dad's name and "Haywood County, Tennessee," where he was born. That's when I uncovered some breaking news: I was the great-great-great grandchild of a Tennessee slave named Sandy Wills.

Sandy was no ordinary slave—he was a freedom fighter! In 1863, he escaped the plantation and took arms to battle against the pro-slavery Confederates in the American Civil War. He joined the Union Army that fought to rid America of slavery once and for all. Still, the Union Army was racially segregated, so Sandy served with free and enslaved black men in the United States Colored Troops division.

Once the Union defeated the Confederates in 1865, Sandy was set free. The tallest, strongest man in his unit, he married a woman named Emma and they had nine children.

Reading the historical records was fascinating, but the more I learned, the more questions I had. It was almost midnight, so I turned off the light and crawled into bed.

Oh, if only I could hear Sandy Wills' voice, [yawn] or see his face, [yawn] or just find a photo [yawn]. That would be… so…so…ama-zing [snore].

I felt a cold hand on my shoulder. I slowly opened my eyes to see this tall, thin man with shiny silver hair hovering over me. He was wearing a dusty blue Civil War uniform with a musket at his side. "Sandy Wills…is…is that you?" I said, rubbing my eyes.

"Yessum, it's me," he said with a strong southern drawl. "I am grateful you woke me up. I haven't slept well these past 126 years."

"I must be dreaming. This is impossible! What's going on here?" I said in total confusion.

"You're the famous reporter—go ahead, ask me whatever you want," he said.

I looked around. I was sitting behind the news desk at my television station and Sandy was pulling out a chair to sit next to me. He looked straight into the TV camera as my producer counted down: three…two…one…ACTION.

"Goo-good morning," I said clumsily. "I'm Cheryl Wills and today I have a very special guest…Sandy Wills. He's umm…he's my…umm…"

"I'm your GREAT-GREAT-GREAT GRANDPA," he said loudly and proudly.

"Yes, of course. Okay," I said clearing my throat. "Grandpa Sandy was a slave who valiantly fought in the Civil War to gain his freedom. So please start by telling our viewers how you came to be a slave."

"I was born into slavery, but I always knew one day I'd be FREE!" he said.

Grandpa Sandy explained that he was a ten-year-old slave boy when two scary-looking men put a sack over his head as he was feeding the chickens. They carried him away screaming and kicking, and they took his mother too. Her piercing cry echoed across the countryside. The two rode on the back of a horse-drawn wagon, up and down the hills of Tipton County, Tennessee.

"The next thing I knew," Grandpa Sandy said, "I was pushed onto an auction block and men were shouting and offering money. I was so confused. I didn't understand what was happening until the auctioneer pointed to me and said, 'SOLD TO EDMUND WILLS FOR $500!' Mama screamed even louder because Master Wills only wanted me, not her."

"I was devastated when I lost my father, but I can't imagine having no parents at all," I said.

"It's a very sad thing for children to suffer such pain," Grandpa Sandy replied. "But I promised Mama right there at the auction that I'd find my way back to her—and I meant it!"

Grandpa Sandy explained that he was forced to take Master Wills' last name. He was then sent to work on the Wills' family plantation in Haywood County, Tennessee.

"At the end of long days picking cotton under the hot Tennessee sun," Grandpa Sandy said, "I found comfort in the hope that Mama's new life was better than mine."

"Did you ever learn to read and write?" I asked.

"Naw," Grandpa Sandy said, recalling the dreadful day Master Wills caught him with a book in his hand.

"I thumbed through it wondering how anyone could deduct words from such strange looking symbols," he explained. "Well, Master Wills stormed across the room and knocked me down. He barked, 'Boy, slaves don't read, they work!'"

"I'm smart, but not literate," Grandpa Sandy said.

Grandpa Sandy made me realize how drastically life has improved for black people in America. In 1863, some states had laws that said enslaved blacks were only three-fifths of a person, that they could be bought and sold like items in a store. Today, African Americans are free to do anything they set their minds to do.

"Did you experience any hopeful times, despite being a slave?" I dared to ask.

"Yes, indeed!" he said. "I hid a handful of hope in my heart and let it all pour out when I was with my friends."

Grandpa Sandy said on Sundays, when no one was allowed to work, he and the boys—James, Andy, Mack, Dick, and Rich—would play together in the vast open fields of the plantation.

"Our favorite game was chasing the birds," he said. "If we managed to slip past one that landed, that meant we were next in line to be freed."

Grandpa Sandy said Rich was the biggest dreamer of all the six boys. Rich imagined himself playing the banjo at wild parties in Memphis, the big city 50 miles south of the plantation.

"Rich would say, 'I'm gonna pluck them banjo strings from dusk to dawn with tunes so sweet the angels'll dance,'" Grandpa Sandy recalled. "Rich said, 'It's just like pickin' cotton!'"

Grandpa Sandy burst into a round of deep-belly laughter. "That good ole Rich always had a plan for what he was going to do and how he was going to do it. He was the freest slave that ever lived!"

"So how did you get off the slave plantation and fight for your freedom?" I asked.

"Glad you asked, Granddaughter!" he exclaimed. "I was 23 years old when I overheard Master Wills telling his business partner that President Abraham Lincoln had signed the Emancipation Proclamation, freeing all of us slaves. Master Wills despised Lincoln and did not regard his new rules. So when the weather warmed up, me and the boys took off by night to Columbus, Kentucky, right over the Tennessee border."

"Was that where you joined the 4th Heavy Field Artillery Unit and battled the Confederate Army?" I asked.

"That's right!" he said with thunderous pride. "Our great leader and abolitionist Frederick Douglass told all black men— slave and free—to take up arms and FIGHT! Douglass said, 'It is better to die FREE than to live as slaves!'"

Life as a soldier was better than slavery, but it wasn't easy, Grandpa Sandy explained.

"Shucks, we didn't even know our left from our right," he said, shaking his head. "When they taught us how to march, they couldn't chant, 'Left. Left. Left, Right, Left.' The officers had to tie a piece of hay to the left leg and a twist of straw to the right and then shout, 'Hay Foot! Straw Foot! Hay Foot! Straw Foot!' That's how we learned to march."

"Did you at least feel respected in the Union Army?" I asked.

"Naw, not at all," Grandpa Sandy said. "The captains in charge called the runaway slaves all kinds of ugly names. But in our hearts, we knew we were smart, good people. We were determined to hold our heads up high and be the best soldiers we could be."

"When the Civil War ended in 1865, I was finally and forever FREE!"
Grandpa Sandy said.

"But it was a bitter and bloody war," he added grimly. "Some 620,000 soldiers died, including good ole Rich."

He pulled a handkerchief from his back pocket and wiped his wet eyes. "Freedom ain't never been free."

"What was the first thing you did after you gained your freedom?" I asked, trying to lighten the mood.

"I made good on my vow!" said Grandpa Sandy, who went back to his hometown in Tipton County to find his mother.

"When Mama saw me, she nearly fainted," he said. "We hugged each other and cried. I was 25, but I was a ten-year-old boy again in sweet Mama's arms."

"How did your life change once you became free?" I asked.

After the war, Grandpa Sandy said he worked as a sharecropper. He met a smart, beautiful young woman named Emma West Moore. They fell in love and the two married soon thereafter. Their first child, William Wills, was born on February 3, 1870.

"I wept when William was born because he was born FREE!" Grandpa Sandy said. "His birth signaled a legacy of freedom for an entire nation. Don't you ever forget that, Granddaughter. Never let the world forget …"

I woke up in a cold sweat and sat straight up. The clock read 2:33 a.m. My computer was glowing in the darkness, so I got up to turn it off. There displayed on the screen was an 1889 newspaper obituary that read:

Sandy Wills, dead at 50.
Former slave from Tipton County, Tennessee,
brave soldier of the Civil War,
loving husband to Emma Wills, and father of nine.

Grandpa hadn't just freed himself and his family tree, but his service in the Union Army helped liberate millions of African Americans who were enslaved in this country.

I knew what I had to do.

I turned on the light and began typing the first chapter of
Die Free: A Heroic Family Tale, a book about my family history.
My mom, brothers, and sisters were thrilled to finally know more
about my father's relatives, even though our last name came from
a slave master. I began traveling all over the world telling
Grandpa Sandy's story—even speaking before representatives
from dozens of countries at the United Nations in New York City.

Now Sandy Wills can rest in peace, knowing that his story is an
inspiration around the world.

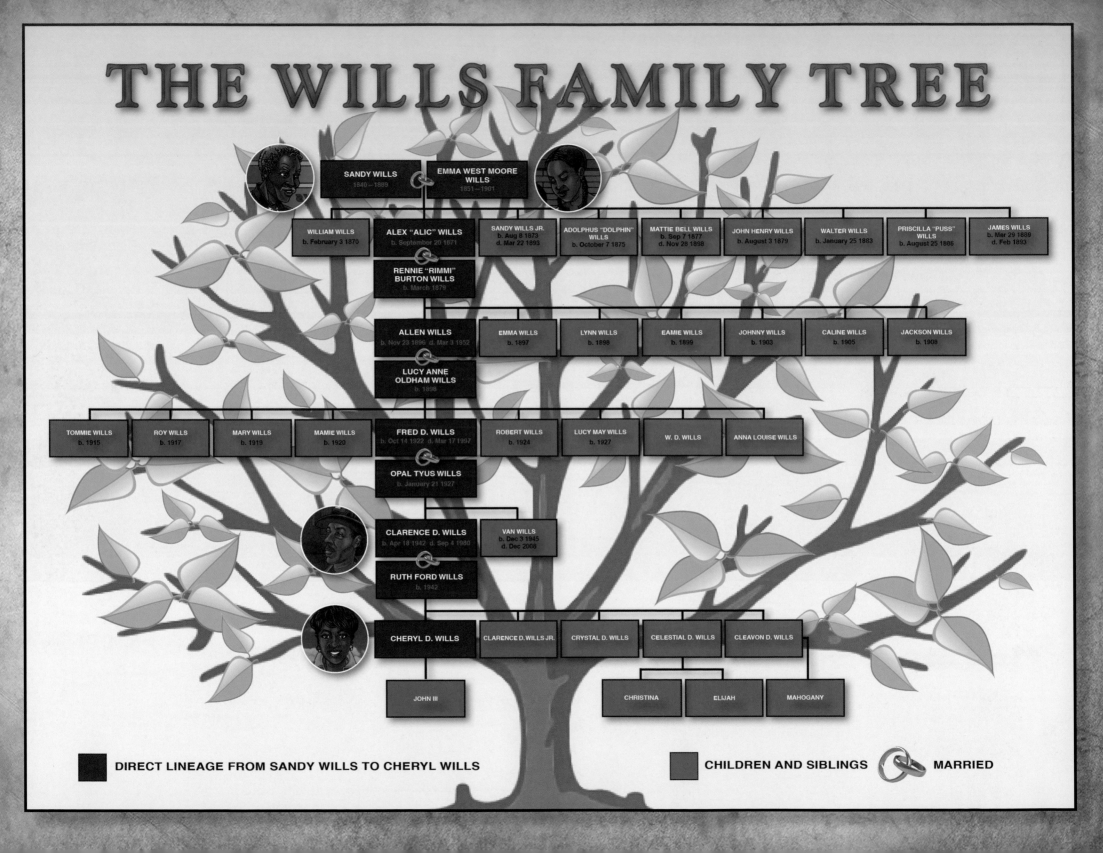

THE WILLS FAMILY TREE

SANDY WILLS 1840 – 1889

EMMA WEST MOORE WILLS 1851 – 1901

WILLIAM WILLS b. February 3 1870	ALEX "ALIC" WILLS b. September 20 1871	SANDY WILLS JR. b. Aug 8 1873 d. Mar 22 1893	ADOLPHUS "DOLPHIN" WILLS b. October 7 1875	MATTIE BELL WILLS b. Sep 7 1877 d. Nov 28 1898	JOHN HENRY WILLS b. August 3 1879	WALTER WILLS b. January 25 1883	PRISCILLA "PUSS" WILLS b. August 25 1886

JAMES WILLS b. Mar 29 1889 d. Feb 1893

RENNIE "RIMMI" BURTON WILLS b. March 1879

ALLEN WILLS b. Nov 23 1896 d. Mar 3 1952	EMMA WILLS b. 1897	LYNN WILLS b. 1898	EAMIE WILLS b. 1899	JOHNNY WILLS b. 1903	CALINE WILLS b. 1905

JACKSON WILLS b. 1908

LUCY ANNE OLDHAM WILLS b. 1898

TOMMIE WILLS b. 1915	ROY WILLS b. 1917	MARY WILLS b. 1919	MAMIE WILLS b. 1920	FRED D. WILLS b. Oct 14 1922 d. Mar 17 1997	ROBERT WILLS b. 1924	LUCY MAY WILLS b. 1927	W. D. WILLS

ANNA LOUISE WILLS

OPAL TYUS WILLS b. January 21 1927

CLARENCE D. WILLS b. Apr 18 1942 d. Sep 4 1980

VAN WILLS b. Dec 3 1945 d. Dec 2006

RUTH FORD WILLS b. 1942

CHERYL D. WILLS	CLARENCE D. WILLS JR.	CRYSTAL D. WILLS	CELESTIAL D. WILLS	CLEAVON D. WILLS

JOHN III

CHRISTINA	ELIJAH	MAHOGANY

■ **DIRECT LINEAGE FROM SANDY WILLS TO CHERYL WILLS**　　　■ **CHILDREN AND SIBLINGS**　　⚭ **MARRIED**

GRANDPA SANDY'S PATH TO FREEDOM

WESTERN KENTUCKY AND TENNESSEE

⬟ **CAPITOL**   ⬡ **COUNTY**   ✿ **CITY**

● ● ● ● ● ● **SANDY'S JOURNEY**

TIPTON COUNTY, TN: Sandy sold at slave auction
HAYWOOD COUNTY, TN: Sandy at Edmund Wills' Plantation
MEMPHIS, TN: Where Rich dreamed of performing
COLUMBUS, KY: Sandy's US military unit

22 miles from Tipton County, TN
to Haywood County, TN
100 miles from Haywood County, TN
to Columbus, KY

▭ **LAKES AND RIVERS**

▲▲▲ **MOUNTAINS**

FRANKFORT

INDIANA

OHIO RIVER

ILLINOIS

POND RIVER

KENTUCKY

TRADEWATER RIVER

KENTUCKY LAKE   LAKE BARKLEY

✿ COLUMBUS

MISSOURI

CUMBERLAND RIVER

OBION LAKE

MISSISSIPPI RIVER

OBION RIVER

DUCK RIVER   ⬟ NASHVILLE

TENNESSEE

⬡ TIPTON   HAYWOOD

BUFFALO RIVER

✿ MEMPHIS

TENNESSEE RIVER

HATCHIE RIVER

WOLF RIVER

MISSISSIPPI   ALABAMA

DEPTH OF KNOWLEDGE TEACHER'S GUIDE

BY VETERAN TEACHER AND EDUCATION BLOGGER MARILYN ANDERSON RHAMES

DISCUSSION QUESTIONS

1) Why do you think some laws in the South deemed black slaves as only three-fifths human?

2) Why do you think Master Wills punished Grandpa Sandy for wanting to learn how to read?

3) Grandpa Sandy said, "I'm smart, but not literate." How can this statement be true?

4) Why was the game about chasing birds so significant to the slave children?

5) In what ways was Rich the "freest slave who ever lived"?

6) How do you feel about Frederick Douglass' statement: "It is better to die as free men than to live as slaves"? Explain.

7) What is the biggest difference between being set free and being born free?

8) What message do you think the author wants you to take away from this book? Why?

EXTENSION ACTIVITIES

1) Make a T-chart of the ways in which Grandpa Sandy was treated like an "item in a store" and as a "person."

2) Use the map at the back of the book to trace the route that Grandpa Sandy and his friends used to escape from Haywood County, TN to Columbus, KY. Write a creative narrative describing what the runaway slaves were thinking; what they said to each other before, during, and after their escape; and include at least three major obstacles they faced along the way.

3) Write a persuasive essay about whether or not author Cheryl Wills should have included Master Edmund Wills in her family tree.

4) Sit down with your guardians, parents, or grandparents and ask them to help you diagram your family tree.

5) You might have a heroic person in your family tree! Ask your parent or guardian to tell you the story, and use research and interviews with that person or other family members to compose a nonfiction account of that person's life.

GLOSSARY

ABOLITIONIST: a person who wants to stop or abolish slavery.

ABRAHAM LINCOLN: 16th president of the United States of America (1861 – 1865). A Republican, his election to the presidency on an anti-slavery platform led to the American Civil War. He was assassinated shortly after the war ended.

AMERICAN CIVIL WAR: war between the northern states (known as the Union) and the Confederate states of the South, 1861–65. The war was fought over the issues of slavery and states' rights. The pro-slavery southern states withdrew from the Union following the election of Abraham Lincoln on an anti-slavery platform, but were defeated by the North.

ANCESTOR: a person who was in someone's family in past times, usually one generation beyond grandparent.

AUCTION BLOCK: a public place where goods were sold to the people who offered the most money.

CONFEDERATE ARMY: the army represented 11 southern states that withdrew from the United States of America and fought in the Civil War to keep slavery intact. This army included men from Alabama, Florida, Georgia, Louisiana, Mississippi, South Carolina, and Texas, and later Arkansas, North Carolina, Tennessee and Virginia. They were defeated by the Union Army.

EMANCIPATION: the process of being set free from legal, social, or political bondage; liberation.

EMANCIPATION PROCLAMATION: declaration made by President Abraham Lincoln during the Civil War on September 22, 1862, freeing all black slaves in the Confederate states. Although Lincoln did not have the power to enforce this declaration, it turned the war into a crusade against slavery. It went into effect on January 1, 1863.

FREDERICK DOUGLASS: prominent American abolitionist, author, and orator. Born a slave, Douglass escaped at age 20 and went on to become a world-renowned anti-slavery activist.

GENEALOGY: the history of a particular family showing how different individuals are related to each other.

LEGACY: a thing or value handed down by someone in the past.

LITERATE: the ability to skillfully read and write.

PLANTATION: a large area of land especially in hot regions where crops (such as cotton) are grown.

UNION ARMY: the army representing 20 states, most in the North, that fought for President Abraham Lincoln in the Civil War against the Confederate Army to end slavery in America. The Union states were Maine, New York, New Hampshire, Vermont, Massachusetts, Connecticut, Rhode Island, Pennsylvania, New Jersey, Ohio, Indiana, Illinois, Kansas, Michigan, Wisconsin, Minnesota, Iowa, California, Nevada, and Oregon. The Union Army ultimately defeated the Confederate Army.

UNITED STATES COLORED TROOPS: regiments of African American soldiers who fought in the Union Army during the Civil War to end slavery. There were 209,000 black Union soldiers.

ACKNOWLEDGMENTS

This book is a labor of love. I would like to thank Ron and Steve Sussman of Lightswitch Learning for believing in this project from the start. I am deeply indebted to our supremely talented illustrator and designer, Randell Pearson for his vision, creativity and fierce commitment to this book. I am also grateful to Marilyn Anderson Rhames for her razor sharp editing and poetic flourishes that melt my heart with every reading. An extra special thank you to Emanuel Robinson for connecting all of the dots as Manager of Operations for Wills Publishing and Productions. And to all of my friends throughout the New York City Department of Education who gave me invaluable advice during the production of this project: Ainsley Rudolfo, Paul Forbes and Shomari Akil. I would like to also acknowledge the numerous organizations who have shown great affection for my story and gave me a platform to tell it: The New York City Police Department, The Council of School Supervisors and Administrators, The United Nations, The United Federation of Teachers, Essence Empowerment Experience, NAACP, New York Association of Black Educators, The Links, Inc., The National Action Network and The United African Congress. Thanks to one and all.

(Pictured above) Widely acclaimed NYC news anchor and author of *The Emancipation of Grandpa Sandy Wills*, Cheryl Wills with the book's illustrator and designer Randell Pearson on the occasion of their initial planning meeting in February 2015. (Pictured on the following endpapers) Men of the United States Colored Troops division who fought in the Civil War.